When David's granddaughter Susan comes to visit him, her day is full of surprises. First, there's a present – but Susan isn't at all sure if she likes it. Then, when she and her grandmother Lisa return from a walk in the forest, there's another, not so pleasant, surprise. Does danger lurk in the tunnel?

British Library Cataloguing in Publication Data

Ainsworth, Alison
    The special present.
    I. Title   II. Series
    823'.914 [J]
    ISBN 0-7214-1261-0

First edition

Published by Ladybird Books Ltd Loughborough Leicestershire UK
Ladybird Books Inc Auburn Maine 04210 USA

Printed in England

The Special Present

David the Gnome

story adaptation by
ALISON AINSWORTH

Ladybird Books

Have you ever wondered who wrote the first fairy tale? Well, perhaps it happened like this.

In the middle of the forest, not far from David's house, lived an old woman and her kitten, Spooky. The old woman wore a long black cloak and had a magic broomstick which carried her over the treetops.

One day Spooky decided to go exploring in the forest. She hadn't gone far when she saw a little girl skipping along, stopping now and then to pick flowers or watch the butterflies.

The little girl's name was Susan, and she was on her way to visit her grandparents. Can you guess who they were? Well, her grandfather was none other than David the Gnome!

Spooky watched as Susan's grandmother came along the path to meet her. "My dear child," she cried, "it's lovely to see you again. And your grandfather is so looking forward to your visit." Spooky – who was a very curious cat – decided to follow them.

When they reached David's house,
Spooky climbed into a tree, and
stretched out on a branch.
Susan ran inside to hug
her grandfather.

"At last! My ray of sunshine!" cried
David. "And I've a present for you!"
Susan's eyes lit up. But when David
handed her a rather dull grey hat, she
felt a bit disappointed. "Thank you," she
said, in a quiet voice.

"But Susan," said Grandmother, "aren't
you pleased with your present? You don't
look very happy."

"Oh, I really like it," replied Susan. "It's just that I've never seen a hat this colour before."

"But it isn't finished yet," laughed Grandfather. "That's the natural colour of the wool. Don't you know how we gnomes make our hats?"

"No, I don't – please tell me!" replied Susan, looking much happier.

"Well, first we go out and collect fur from deer that are losing their winter coats," explained Grandfather, "or rabbits' wool that has caught on fences and hedges."

"But how do you *colour* the hats?" Susan wanted to know.

"Come and I'll show you," said Grandmother. "I haven't dyed your hat yet because I didn't know what colour you wanted."

"I've always wanted a red hat!" cried Susan.

"Then that's the colour your hat shall be!" said Grandmother. "All our dyes come from plants and berries," she explained when they were outside. "We get blue from indigo plants, yellow from columbine, and red from hemp juice."

Grandmother put the hat in a wooden tub full of red dye and set to work. When she had finished, Susan's hat was bright scarlet. It looked really splendid.

She rushed inside to show Grandfather.

"My word, Susan, you look as pretty as a princess!" he exclaimed. "Why don't you and your grandmother go for a walk to show off your new hat?"

By this time, Spooky had fallen asleep in the tree, so she didn't see Susan and her grandmother as they set off on their walk.

Grandmother knew the names of all the pretty flowers that grew along the path, and there were so many wild creatures to see – squirrels, rabbits, mice, baby deer and all sorts of birds.

The hours flew by. Then Grandmother said, "It's getting late – we should be going home now. Your grandfather will be worrying about us."

"Why don't we ask Swift to take us home?" asked Susan. She sent a bluebird to fetch Swift, who was only too happy to help. With Susan and Grandmother on his back, he raced through the forest, leaping over streams and rocks, and in no time at all they had arrived home.

Spooky, who had been sleeping peacefully, woke up when she heard the sound of Swift's paws on the ground. She jumped down from the tree, and was about to run home, when Swift appeared.

Spooky was terrified at the sight of the fox, and she ran straight down the tunnel leading to David's home. Suddenly the ground gave way beneath her and she felt herself falling. Then everything went black.

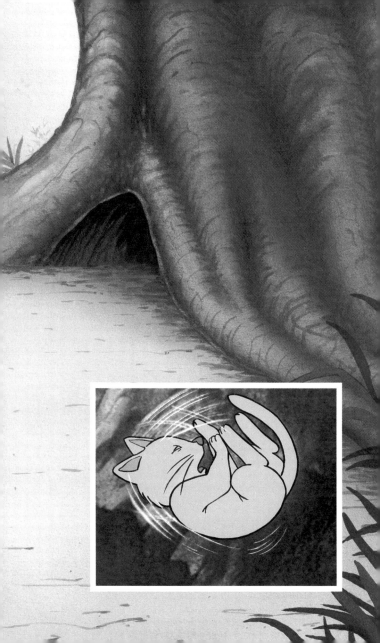

Susan and her grandmother slipped off Swift's back, and were walking through the tunnel, when they heard a crying sound under their feet.

"What's that noise?" asked Susan.

"We have an entrance trap in the ground just here," replied Grandmother. "It's to stop small creatures getting into the house." She lifted the heavy trapdoor and they peered in. Peering back at them was the kitten!

Before they could say anything, Spooky jumped up out of the trap and made for the tunnel entrance.

Swift was sitting just outside. When he heard a scampering noise in the tunnel, he looked inside to see what was coming. At first, when Spooky saw what looked like a huge wolf's head, she was too frightened to come out.

Then with a defiant "miaow", she
dashed out of the tunnel past Swift, and
ran as fast as her short little legs could
carry her.

When she reached the safety of her cottage, Spooky told the old woman all about her adventures.

"That would make a good story," thought the old woman. And she started to write in a big black book.

"Hmm, now let me see," she muttered to herself. "A little girl in a red hat, going to visit her grandmother in the forest… where she meets a big bad wolf…" She scribbled furiously. "I know!" she cried. "I'll call the story 'Little Red Riding Hood'!"

Before she went to sleep that night, Susan asked Grandmother to read her a fairy tale.

"Do you know where fairy tales come from, Grandmother?" she asked.

Lisa shook her head. "Well, my dear, I don't know who made up all those foolish tales about witches and fierce wolves living in the forest. Forests may appear to be mysterious places, especially at night, but gnomes have nothing to do with such silly ideas. We're far too sensible for that. Now off to sleep!"

And soon Susan was fast asleep, dreaming about her lovely red hat, the ride with Swift and the little cat.

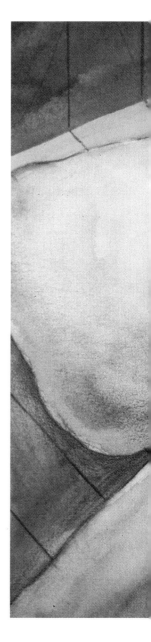